It's a Fiesta, Benjamin

Other Yearling Books by Patricia Reilly Giff you will enjoy:

The Polk Street Specials
Write Up a Storm with the Polk Street School
Count Your Money with the Polk Street School
The Postcard Pest
Turkey Trouble
Look Out, Washington, D.C.!

The Kids of the Polk Street School books
The Beast in Ms. Rooney's Room
The Candy Corn Contest
Lazy Lions, Lucky Lambs
In the Dinosaur's Paw
Purple Climbing Days
and more

The Lincoln Lions Band books
Meet the Lincoln Lions Band
Yankee Doodle Drumsticks
The Jingle Bells Jam
The Rootin' Tootin' Bugle Boy
The Red, White, and Blue Valentine
The Great Shamrock Disaster

YEARLING BOOKS are designed especially to entertain and enlighten young people. Patricia Reilly Giff, consultant to this series, received her bachelor's degree from Marymount College and a master's degree in history from St. John's University. She holds a Professional Diploma in Reading and a Doctorate of Humane Letters from Hofstra University. She was a teacher and reading consultant for many years, and is the author of numerous books for young readers.

For a complete listing of all Yearling titles, write to
Dell Readers Service, P.O. Box 1045,
South Holland, IL 60473.

Friends
and Amigos

6

It's a Fiesta, Benjamin

Patricia Reilly Giff

ILLUSTRATED BY
DyAnne DiSalvo-Ryan

A Yearling Book

Published by
Bantam Doubleday Dell Books for Young Readers
a division of
Bantam Doubleday Dell Publishing Group, Inc.
1540 Broadway
New York, New York 10036

If you purchased this book without a cover you should be aware that this book is stolen property. It was reported as "unsold and destroyed" to the publisher and neither the author nor the publisher has received any payment for this "stripped book."

Text copyright © 1996 by Patricia Reilly Giff
Illustrations copyright © 1996 by DyAnne DiSalvo-Ryan

All rights reserved. No part of this book may be reproduced or transmitted in any form or by any means, electronic or mechanical, including photocopying, recording, or by any information storage and retrieval system, without the written permission of the Publisher, except where permitted by law.

The trademarks Yearling® and Dell® are registered in the U.S. Patent and Trademark Office and in other countries.

ISBN: 0-440-41089-4

Printed in the United States of America

June 1996
10 9 8 7 6 5 4 3 2
CWO

To
June McAllister,
with love

Where to Find the Spanish Lessons in This Book

It's a Fiesta, Benjamin

BENJAMIN'S SPANISH NOTES

El apartamento de la señora Sanchez (ehl ah-pahr-tah-MEHN-toh deh lah seh-NYOH-rah SAHN-chehs)	Mrs. Sanchez's Apartment
sala (SAH-lah)	living room
sofá (so-FAH)	couch
mesa (MEH-sah)	table
televisor (teh-leh-vee-SOHR)	television set
ver televisión (VEHR teh-leh-vee-SYOHN)	to watch television
pintura (peen-TOO-rah)	painting
silla (SEE-yah)	chair
ventana (ven-TAH-nah)	window

1

It was hot. Sticky. And Benjamin Bean was late.

He yanked his dresser drawer open. He pulled out a clean T-shirt.

"Don't forget to wash," his mother called.

Too late for the clean T-shirt.

He raced into the bathroom.

He stuck his head under the faucet.

It was cold. Wonderful.

He dashed into the kitchen.

"Ready?" his mother asked.

He looked at his little brother, Adam.

Adam was the worst mess. Ketchup on his face. Chocolate pudding on his nose.

"I'm not going with Adam looking like that," Benjamin said.

"No time to get him changed," his mother said. "Take him with you. Daddy and I will be down in a few minutes."

Adam put a fire hat on his head. It almost covered his eyes.

He stood in front of the door.

"No good," Benjamin said. "Wait for Mom and Dad."

"Yes good," said Adam. "I'm coming."

Benjamin sighed. "Don't say a word when we get there."

Adam was always saying things he shouldn't . . . things he thought were funny . . . things Benjamin thought were terrible.

Benjamin hurried out the door with Adam.

"Hold my hand," he said when they reached the stairs. "We have to hurry."

"No good." Adam sat on the top step. He bumped his way down.

It took forever to get to the second floor.

Benjamin could hear the noise before they reached the bottom step.

Señora Sanchez's door was open.

It seemed as if the whole world were in her living room.

All the neighbors. Mrs. Halfpenny, Benjamin's teacher. Mrs. Muñoz, the librarian.

Mannie, from the bakery. Benjamin's friends Sarah and Anna, and Erica and Thomas Attonichi, and—

"Too many people," Adam said. He grabbed Benjamin's hand.

Adam's hand was sticky with juice, or jelly, or maybe lollipop.

Señora Sanchez spotted them. "Adam," she called. "And Benjamin."

It sounded like Ben-hah-MEEN.

Benjamin smiled at her.

Señora Sanchez was a wonderful artist. She had come to Springfield Gardens in October. She had learned English, and now she was teaching him Spanish.

Right now, one of her paintings was propped up on her table.

It showed a pool . . . a pool so real Benjamin felt like jumping in.

He looked closer.

In the painting, a tiny Benjamin really was jumping in.

His friends Anna and Sarah were jumping in, too.

"Great news." Señora Sanchez waved her arms around. "This summer, we'll have a *piscina* on Spring Street."

"Pee-SEE-nah: That means pool!" cried Anna.

Everyone began to clap. *¡Qué maravilloso!*

"But what about money?" someone asked.

Adam jumped around in his fire hat.

"Stop," Benjamin told him.

"Benjamin didn't change his shirt," Adam said.

No one was listening, though. Everyone was talking about the pool . . . and how much it would cost.

Señora Sanchez was nodding. "We'll have a *fiesta*," she said, "to help pay for it."

Everyone was clapping again . . . and eating Señora Sanchez's *torta*.

The cake had a strange taste, Benjamin thought.

"I didn't cook it long enough," Señora Sanchez whispered to him.

Everyone was planning. Who would bake?

Mannie, the baker, raised his hand. "I make the best tortillas," he said.

And who would string the lights?

"I'll do the lights," Mr. Bean said as he walked in the door.

And who would make signs . . . and play music . . . and who would put on a dance show?

"Sarah and I will dance," Anna said. "My mother will teach us."

"*Maravilloso,*" Señora Sanchez said. "A dance is *importante* in a festival."

"Wonderful," Anna's mother said. "I have some old costumes . . . *vestuario* . . . from Colombia."

"And one more thing," said Señora Sanchez. "We need a *limpieza.*"

Anna's mother smiled. "Yes."

"Who will—" Señora Sanchez began.

"Benjamin," said Adam from under his fire hat.

Benjamin shook his head.

He didn't even know what a *limpieza* was.

Everyone was looking at them.

Adam was saying something else. "Benjamin doesn't change his under—"

Benjamin opened his mouth wide. "Yes," he said before Adam could finish. "I'll do the *limpieza*."

BENJAMIN'S SPANISH NOTES

El baile *(ehl BAAEE-leh)*	**Dance**
bailarín *(baaee-lah-REEN)*	dancer (boy)
bailarina *(baaee-lah-REE-nah)*	dancer (girl)
bailarinas *(baaee-lah-REE-nahs)*	dancers (girls)
pareja *(pah-REH-hah)*	partner
vestuario *(vehs-tooAH-reeoh)*	costumes
música *(MOO-see-kah)*	music
tambor *(tahm-BOHR)*	drum
pasos *(PAH-sohs)*	steps
ensayo *(ehn-SAH-yoh)*	rehearsal

2

Benjamin was sitting in Anna's backyard.

Anna's mother, Mrs. Ortiz, had just brought out a tray of lemonade.

The lemonade needed a ton of sugar, Benjamin thought.

The ice cubes were *maravillosos.*

Next to him, Adam was running an ice cube over his face. It was making clean paths on his dirty face.

Benjamin wanted to tell him to stop. But

Adam would probably tell everyone that he hadn't taken a bath today.

Music was blaring from the Ortiz kitchen.

"Music from Colombia," Mrs. Ortiz said.

Benjamin didn't want to think about music.

It was too hot to think about anything except diving into the new pool on Spring Street.

He didn't know how Sarah and Anna could be sitting there in long skirts, with tons of ruffles all over them.

He couldn't wait for the fiesta . . . and the money to build the *piscina*, and—

"Pay attention, Benjamin," Sarah said, swirling her skirt around. "We're trying to tell you—"

"What?" he said.

"Benjamin didn't take—" Adam began.

"Be quiet, Adam," said Benjamin.

Anna broke in. "We need you for the *baile*."

Benjamin looked up. "Me? Don't be silly."

"Didn't take—" Adam began again.

Sarah sighed. "If you'd only listen," she said. "You don't have to dance."

"No," Anna said. "You just have to play the drums."

"Didn't take a bath," said Adam.

Sarah looked down at him. "What's that kid talking about?"

"Never mind."

"Drums, Benjamin," Anna said. "We need you."

Benjamin swallowed his ice cube. He

couldn't play the drums in a thousand years. "I don't know how," he said.

Anna narrowed her eyes. "Don't be a *chivo*."

"That means goat, in case you're interested," Sarah said. "Anyone can play the drums. *Pahm de pam pam*."

"*Pa pahm!*" Adam screamed. He jumped down Anna's three back steps.

All he had on were sneakers, the fire hat, and a pair of striped shorts.

"Guess what else about Benjie's dog," he said when he landed.

Benjamin opened his mouth. His dog, Perro, wasn't exactly housebroken. He could just guess what Adam would say next.

"Don't say a word," he told Adam. "If you open your mouth one more time . . ."

Sarah fanned her face with her hand. "*¡Qué calor!*" she said. "Wasn't Señora Sanchez wonderful to think of the *fiesta* and the *piscina*?"

"We ought to do something for her," Anna said. "Something—"

"*Maravilloso,*" said Benjamin. He'd really love to do something for Señora Sanchez. She was the best grown-up friend he had ever had.

Just then, Mrs. Ortiz came outside.

She handed Adam two maracas. "Shake these up and down," she said. Then she snapped her fingers. "Oops. I forgot the drum."

She disappeared into the house again.

"Listen," Benjamin told Sarah and Anna. "I can't play the drums. Besides, I'm doing the *limpieza.*"

Anna shook her head and laughed. "I forgot about the *limpieza*. Never mind. You'll be finished with the *limpieza* by the weekend. You have plenty of time to learn. . . ."

Benjamin wasn't listening.

He had to keep staring at Adam so that he wouldn't talk.

At the same time, he wondered whether to ask what a *limpieza* was.

Anna would call him a *chivo*.

Sarah would laugh.

They'd both think he was crazy for saying he'd do it when he didn't even—

Mrs. Ortiz banged out the back door. "I can't find it anywhere," she said. "Look around for a couple of sticks. Just for now we'll make believe. . . ."

Benjamin was shaking his head. "I can't. . . ."

Mrs. Ortiz smiled. "Anyone who is willing to do a *limpieza* can certainly play a drum."

Adam looked up. "What's a *limpieza*?"

Mrs. Ortiz took a sip of lemonade. "It's a cleanup. In Ecuador, the whole street is cleaned the week before the festival. Papers picked up, old leaves, everything swept."

Benjamin stood up. It was almost too hot to move.

He tried to look as if he had known what a *limpieza* was all along.

He couldn't believe he was going to clean the whole street.

Adam's fault.

Adam was talking about the dog again.

Benjamin was too hot to try to stop him.

BENJAMIN'S SPANISH NOTES

El barrio (ehl BAH-rreeoh)	The Neighborhood
acera (ah-SEH-rah)	sidewalk
calle (KAH-yeh)	street
avenida (ah-veh-NEE-dah)	avenue
cuadra (KWAH-drah)	block
esquina (ehs-KEE-nah)	corner

3

The thermometer outside said ninety. It was the hottest day of the year.

Benjamin wiped sweat off his forehead. He watched Señora Sanchez.

She was standing in the middle of Spring Street.

She was wearing beads, and earrings, and an old straw hat.

It was lucky Benjamin didn't have to do the *limpieza* by himself.

All the other kids were going to help Señora Sanchez, too.

They were sitting on the curb. Sarah and
her sister, Erica; Anna; and Thomas.

They were staring at Adam, trying not to
laugh.

Adam was still wearing the fire hat. And
today he was clumping around in his father's boots.

Señora Sanchez didn't pay attention to
the laughing. "Good to put the fire out,"
she said. *"Fuego."*

Adam was racing down the street.
"Fire!" he yelled. *"¡FoooEHHH-goh!"*

It was a good thing cars almost never
came up Spring Street, Benjamin thought.
Adam would be peanut butter.

The dogs chased around after Adam.

Benjamin's dog, Perro, was barking. Sarah's yellow dog, Gus, was, too.

Bonita, Señora Sanchez's dog, was bouncing around like a tennis ball.

It was too hot to move, Benjamin thought.

"*Limpieza,*" Señora Sanchez was saying. It was hard to hear her over the noise.

"Say *leem-PYEH-sah,*" Benjamin told Adam.

Adam didn't answer.

He was sucking on a fat green lollipop.

"*Limpieza* happens in Ecuador in November," Señora Sanchez said.

Benjamin looked down. He could see four wads of bubble gum stuck to the curb.

And papers.

His papers, and Sarah's.

He smiled, thinking about it.

They had been so glad the math test was over, they had flown the papers down the street.

"Don't worry," he had told Sarah. "I'll pick them up, shove them right in the apartment garbage."

"If one person ever sees my math mark . . . ," Sarah had begun.

Right now, Benjamin leaned over. In front of him was a ripped paper.

BENJAMIN BEAN, it said on top in his handwriting.

EXCELLENT . . . BUT SLOPPY! in Mrs. Halfpenny's.

Benjamin covered the writing with his foot.

He wondered where Sarah's paper was.

Maybe he should have thrown them away.

He didn't even remember why he hadn't.

Next to him, Adam put his lollipop on the curb.

Benjamin could see that he was chewing on a piece of gum.

"Where did you get that?" Benjamin asked.

He knew the answer, though. "Spit it out, Adam. You're going to get a horrible disease."

Adam poked Anna. "I think Benjamin sucks his thumb," he said.

"I do not," Benjamin said.

But Anna was bending over. She was looking at one of the papers flying around.

"Fourteen mistakes," she said.

He looked down at it.

The top of the paper with the name had been torn off. But he knew it was Sarah's.

Anna grinned at him. "I bet this is yours, *chivo.*"

He shook his head. "No, it isn't."

"Fourteen mistakes!" Anna said. "I thought you were so good in math."

"It's not mine," Benjamin said before he could think. "It's Sarah's."

Just then, Señora Sanchez handed them trash bags and work gloves.

"Wait until Sarah sees this," Anna said. She pulled on one of the work gloves. "She's going to laugh."

"Don't . . . ," Benjamin began. He knew Sarah wouldn't laugh.

He was right. She looked as if she was going to cry.

"Fourteen mistakes," Anna was telling her. She waved the paper around.

Benjamin looked for Señora Sanchez.

But she was at the other end of the street.

"That's a lot of mistakes," Anna said, laughing.

Sarah put her nose up close to Anna's. "You went poking through the garbage? And you're the worst in the class in spelling," she said. "And everybody knows it."

Anna stepped back. Her cheeks turned pink. *"Estúpida,"* she told Sarah.

"Bebé," said Sarah.

"Don't fight . . . ," Benjamin was saying.

Too late.

They both took off for home.

Benjamin and Señora Sanchez were left with Thomas Attonichi, who still hadn't gotten off the curb; Sarah's little sister, Erica; and Adam, who was pretending to put out a fire.

"*Caramba,*" Señora Sanchez said.

"Double *caramba,*" said Benjamin.

BENJAMIN'S SPANISH NOTES

La limpieza (lah leem-PYEH-sah)	The Cleanup
cubo (KOO-boh)	bucket
escoba (ehs-KOH-bah)	broom
detergente (deh-tehr-HEHN-teh)	detergent
toalla (toh-AH-yah)	towel
basura (bah-SOO-rah)	garbage
basurero (bah-soo-REH-roh)	trash can
trapeador (trah-peh-ah-DOHR)	mop
limpio (LEEM-peeoh)	clean
sucio (SOO-seeoh)	dirty

4

It was after supper.

Benjamin could hear hammering outside on Spring Street.

It was the cleanest street in Springfield Gardens.

Right now his father was building a stand to show Señora Sanchez's artwork. And Mannie, the baker, was starting a food stand for his tortillas.

Benjamin thought about the *fiesta* while he crawled around on the living-room floor.

He was trying to put his train tracks together.

Adam had pulled them apart again. Then he had fallen asleep on the engine.

Benjamin looked at him for a moment.

Adam looked like a great kid when he was asleep.

Outside, their father must have hit his thumb with the hammer.

Benjamin could hear him yell.

There was another sound, too, the sound of Señora Sanchez banging on the fire escape with her dustpan.

It was her signal.

She was looking for him.

Benjamin was up in a flash, racing for the window.

Adam was up, too. "Take me . . . take me, Benjie."

"Take the stairs," his mother called after him.

It was too late.

Benjamin opened the screen.

He clattered down the fire escape.

Behind him, Adam was screaming, "Please, take me, too, Benjie. Please . . ."

Benjamin was still high enough to see the back of Sarah's house across the trees.

Sarah was sitting on her steps with her dog, Gus.

She was leaning on her elbows.

Benjamin stopped.

Even from here, she looked sad.

It was probably about her fight with Anna.

He watched her for a minute.

Suddenly his mouth was dry.

Suppose Sarah and Anna didn't talk to each other all week.

What would happen to the dance for the *fiesta*? And all the games they had planned?

Señora Sanchez poked her head out of her window. On her cheek was a dab of pink paint.

"Benjamin," she called.

He took the last few steps to her apartment window, ducked his head, and went inside.

The picture of the blue pool was still on the table.

Another picture was there, too. A picture of the *fiesta*.

Spring Street was crowded. People were watching Sarah and Anna dance.

Señora Sanchez was painting a clown face on Erica. And kids were playing games.

Benjamin looked at the easel in the corner.

Señora Sanchez waved her hand. "I'm working on a painting," she said. "*Mi prima.* My cousin. Mercedes Estévez."

Benjamin looked at the picture of Mercedes.

She had a wisp of hair over one ear. Her pink eyeglasses were crooked.

She looked as if she were going to laugh any minute.

"She lives in Spanish Harlem . . . not so far," Señora Sanchez said. "If I could see her for . . . just for a minute . . ."

She shook her head. "We had a little argument—*una disputa.* The silliest fight . . . over how to make empanadas. Now we don't call each other. We don't speak."

Señora Sanchez sighed. She went into the

kitchen and came back with a bowl of pop-corn.

It looked a little burned.

"Palomitas de maíz," she told Benjamin. She stuck a piece in his mouth and one in Bonita's.

"La familia es muy importante." She tried to smile. "And *amigos*, too.

"Now," she said. "About the *fiesta*. Mrs. Halfpenny made signs. Many signs. They invite everyone to the *fiesta*."

She pushed the popcorn bowl toward him. "Everyone will help give them out. *¿Sí?* You, and Sarah, and Anna, and—"

Benjamin swallowed. "I think Sarah and Anna are still fighting."

"It's sad when two friends have a *disputa*," Señora Sanchez said. "But you will fix it, Benjamin. I know you will."

She leaned forward. "You must fix it. Otherwise, I think the *fiesta* will be spoiled."

Benjamin nodded a little.

He took the signs in his hands and looked down at them.

He couldn't begin to think of a way to make them friends again.

But Señora Sanchez was right. Somehow they had to make up.

BENJAMIN'S SPANISH NOTES

La familia *(lah fah-MEE-leeah)*	Family
los parientes *(lohs pah-RYEHN-tehs)*	relatives
los hijos *(lohs EE-hohs)*	sons and daughters
los hermanos *(lohs ehr-MAH-nohs)*	brothers; brothers and sisters
la hermana *(lah ehr-MAH-nah)*	sister
el hermano *(ehl ehr-MAH-noh)*	brother
los papás *(lohs pah-PAHS)*	parents
los abuelos *(lohs ah-booEH-lohs)*	grandparents
los primos *(lohs PREE-mohs)*	cousins

5

"One sign for the library," Benjamin told himself as he finished breakfast. "One for the bakery. One at the corner, and one . . ."

Adam was standing on the kitchen table. He was holding a spray bottle of water. "I'm putting out the fire," he was yelling to Perro, the dog. "Don't worry."

Their mother pushed her hair back off her forehead. "It must be a hundred degrees in here," she said. "How about taking Adam with you?"

Benjamin frowned. "Anna is waiting for me right this minute."

Adam frowned, too. "Benjamin didn't brush—" he began.

Benjamin took a breath. Brush his teeth? Brush the dog? He hadn't done either one.

He didn't wait for Adam to finish.

"All right," he said. "But hurry."

Adam smiled. "You're good, Benjie."

Adam raced out the door. He was already bumping down the stairs when Benjamin got there.

And Anna was waiting outside. "We'll give out a hundred of these guys," she said. "A thousand."

"Really?" Adam asked.

"Maybe ten or twelve," Benjamin said.

They walked down Spring Street.

Benjamin's father had finished the art stand. And Mannie had finished the bakery stand.

Mrs. Muñoz, the librarian, was rolling a cart along the street. "I had a great idea," she told them. "I'm going to sell books at the *fiesta* on Saturday."

Benjamin nodded and kept going.

There was a lot to do today . . . give out signs . . . and talk Anna into making up with Sarah.

Adam was standing still, though. "I want to see the books," he said.

Mrs. Muñoz smiled. "It's just the cart," she said. "I want to see if it fits here under the trees."

"You know what?" Adam said.

"Let's go," Benjamin told him.

"What?" Mrs. Muñoz asked.

"It's about Benjamin," Adam said.

Anna began to laugh. "Uh-oh," she said.

Benjamin hitched the signs up higher under his arm. "I'm going without you," he told Adam.

"Bye," Adam told Mrs. Muñoz.

They turned the corner. "You're a pain," he told Adam. "The worst tattletale."

Adam stuck out his lower lip. "I am not."

Benjamin didn't pay attention. He had to talk to Anna . . . had to talk to her right now.

He cleared his throat. "How's the dance, the *baile,* coming?"

Anna shook her head. "No *baile.* No nothing—*nada.*"

Benjamin leaned a little closer. "Maybe you should tell Sarah you're sorry."

Anna looked sad for a moment. Then she narrowed her eyes. "And maybe not. Sarah said I was terrible in spelling."

She stopped for a breath. "She said I was a garbage picker. How could she say that?"

"But . . . ," he began.

Anna didn't answer. She grabbed a sign. She dived into the fish store with it.

A moment later she was back. "He'll put it in the window," she said.

"I really think you should make up with Sarah," Benjamin said. "She felt bad about the—"

"Don't be a *chivo*," Anna cut in. She took another sign and went into Moy's Chinese Restaurant.

Outside again, she put her hand on top of her head. "I'm burning up," she said. "I can't wait for the *piscina*."

"Maybe there won't be a *piscina*," Benjamin said, "if there isn't any *baile*."

Anna closed her mouth in a thin line. "We should do something nice for Señora Sanchez," she said.

Benjamin nodded. "But what?"

They turned the corner.

He looked back. "Adam?"

His mouth was dry.

"Where's Adam?" he asked.

"Maybe he's hiding?" Anna said.

Benjamin started back. There was no place to hide.

Only a few trees. A few stores.

Adam was gone.

FIESTA ESPAÑOLA
sábado el 28 de junio

TORTILLAS
AGUA DE PANELA
PALOMITAS DE MAÍZ
AND MORE!

fiesta *(FYEHS-tah)*	party
española *(ehs-pah-NYOH-lah)*	Spanish
sábado *(SAH-bah-doh)*	Saturday
el 28 de junio *(ehl vehyn-teeOH-choh deh HOO-nyoh)*	June 28
comida *(koh-MEE-dah)*	food
música *(MOO-see-kah)*	music
baile *(BAAee-leh)*	dance
juegos *(hooEH-gohs)*	games

6

Benjamin sped down the street.

"Adam!" he yelled. His voice sounded strange. Almost scared.

He was scared.

He headed for home. His mother would know what to do.

Then he remembered.

His mother was going to buy flowerpots for the *fiesta*.

Where was Adam?

He could hear Anna calling Adam from the next block.

Sarah was coming down the street.

Benjamin could hardly open his mouth.

Sarah stopped. She looked at his face. "What's the matter?"

"Adam's lost."

"No," Sarah said. "I just saw him two minutes ago."

Benjamin looked up and down the street. "Where?"

"Near the bakery." She waved her hand. "I was surprised. I didn't think your mother would let him out alone."

Benjamin's mouth was dry. The bakery.

Adam would have had to cross Higby Avenue.

Benjamin closed his eyes.

He started down the street.

By the time they reached the corner, they were running.

Sarah's little sister, Erica, was standing in front of the bakery.

Anna came barreling down the street from the other side. "I can't find him anywhere."

"Adam . . . ?" Benjamin asked Erica, out of breath.

Erica took a bite of the tortilla she was eating. "Mannie's going to make these for the *fiesta*."

"What about Adam?" Benjamin asked.

He thought about the other night. Adam crying, "Take me with you."

Adam asleep on the model train engine in the living room.

Erica took the last bite. She wiped her mouth on her arm.

"Answer him, Erica," Sarah said.

"Adam ran away. He's never going home again."

Erica opened the bakery door. "I'm going to get another one of those tortilla things."

She looked back over her shoulder. "I don't know where he's going to live."

Sarah grabbed Erica's ponytail. "Where is Adam now?"

"He's hiding," Erica said, walking backward. "I'm not supposed to tell."

"But why?" Anna asked.

"That's what I want to know," said Sarah.

Erica rolled her eyes. "Because of Benjamin."

"Benjamin?" Sarah asked.

"Me?" Benjamin said. He could hear his voice squeaking.

Anna and Sarah began to laugh. Then they remembered they were fighting.

Sarah looked through the bakery window.

Anna stared down at her sneakers.

"I have to find him right now," Benjamin said. "I have to bring him home before my mother . . ."

Erica didn't say anything. She pointed toward the bakery.

"Inside?" Benjamin asked.

He didn't wait for an answer.

He pushed open the door, said hello to Mannie, and went toward the back.

Erica's mother was standing at a large table.

She was sifting sugar over little cakes. "I'll pop these in the freezer," she said. "They'll be wonderful for the *fiesta*."

She smiled at Benjamin and moved her head a little.

Adam was sitting there, under the table, covering his eyes.

"Try a little cake," Sarah's mother told Benjamin.

Benjamin sank down on the stool and sighed.

Sometimes he was mean to Adam.

He looked around.

Sarah and Erica were standing there.

But Anna hadn't even come into the bakery.

He thought about Anna and Sarah, and the papers flying around the street.

Then he realized.

Their fight was all his fault, too.

If he had thrown the papers away in the first place . . . if he hadn't told Anna it was Sarah's paper. If . . .

What was he going to do now?

¿Dónde está Adam?

¡Socorro!

Do you know what these sentences mean?

1. La piscina es maravillosa.
2. Los amigos son muy importantes.
3. Me gusta la música.
4. La fiesta es divertida.
5. ¿Dónde está Adam?

Where Is Adam?

Help!

Translation

1. The pool is marvelous.
2. Friends are very important.
3. I like music.
4. The party is fun.
5. Where is Adam?

7

Benjamin was sitting on his windowsill.
He could see one of their *fiesta* signs on the
telephone pole.

He could see across to Sarah's house, too,
and behind that, one corner of Anna's blue
roof.

Everything was quiet.

It was too early for anyone to be awake.

Even Adam was asleep under his sheet,
his thumb in his mouth.

It had taken a long time to get Adam out from under the bakery table yesterday.

When he had crawled out, he had told Benjamin he was going to live in the Higby Avenue railroad station.

He was going to get breakfast from the candy machine.

He was going to sleep in the waiting room.

"You'll miss the *fiesta*," Benjamin had said. "You'll miss the *comida*, and the *juegos*, and the *música*, and the *baile* . . . and the ride on the fire truck."

Erica had given Adam a tortilla. "Maybe you'd better go home after all."

Benjamin looked at Adam now.

"I'm a tattletale," Adam had told Benjamin in the bakery.

He had said it looking down at the floor.

Benjamin hadn't even been sure he had heard him.

"Don't worry," Erica had said. "Eat your tortilla. You won't tattle anymore."

Benjamin had to smile.

Adam had started to tattle four times after they had gotten home last night. But each time he had clapped his hands over his mouth.

Now, in the morning, Benjamin watched his father come outside.

A string of Christmas lights was in his hands.

He was going to string them all over Spring Street for the *fiesta*.

Benjamin heard Sarah's back door open. He saw Sarah talking to Erica.

He sighed.

He knew he had to tell Sarah what he had done . . . that he was a worse tattletale than Adam.

He stood up.

But then he smelled something burning.

He could hear Señora Sanchez shouting.

"*¡Caramba!*" she shrieked.

It was a good thing Benjamin was wearing the birthday pajamas from his grandmother.

They were the best ones he had.

He pushed the screen up and crawled out on the fire escape.

Down below, Señora Sanchez's window was wide open.

Smoke was pouring out.

Benjamin raced down the fire escape.

He stopped at Señora Sanchez's window.

There was less smoke now. But something smelled awful.

Señora Sanchez was waving a mat. "*Caramba*," she said again.

She looked up and saw Benjamin in his purple pajamas.

"*¡Me gusta tu pijama!*" she said. "*Maravilloso pijama*. I like *púrpura*. Purple."

Benjamin slid into the kitchen through the open window.

He looked around.

Smoke was coming from the frying pan on the stove.

Señora Sanchez waved her hands around. "My empanadas are ruined. I looked away for one minute. I wanted to paint a necklace on Mercedes. And *poof!*"

Benjamin looked at the mess on the stove.

It would take forever to clean the pan.

And even though it was early, the kitchen was steaming hot.

Señora Sanchez was fanning her face with her apron. "What will I do about the empanadas?"

Benjamin swallowed. *"¡No pasó nada!"* he said. "I'll get everyone to help. Me and Anna, and Erica." He stopped. "And Adam. I'll even get Sarah, too . . . somehow."

Ingredientes (een-greh-deeEHN-tehs)	Ingredients
relleno (reh-YEH-noh)	filling
frutas (FROO-tahs)	fruit
pollo (POH-yoh)	chicken
carne (KAHR-neh)	meat
jamón (hah-MOHN)	ham
cantidades (kahn-tee-DAH-dehs)	amounts (quantities)
una taza de . . . (OO-nah TAH-sah deh)	one cup of . . .
una taza y media . . . (OO-nah TAH-sah EE MEH- dyah)	one and a half cups . . .
un huevo (OON ooEH-voh)	one egg
una cucharadita (OO-nah koo-chah-rah-DEE- tah)	one teaspoonful

There wasn't an inch of space left on Señora Sanchez's kitchen table.

Bowls of chopped meat, a rolling pin,
milk, eggs, apples, and peaches were
crowded together.

Anna was standing at the counter, sifting
flour. Her hands were white, and so was her
nose.

Señora Sanchez lifted Adam up on a stool
to watch.

Sarah wasn't watching Anna, though. "Benjamin didn't tell me you'd be here," she said without looking at Anna.

Anna wiped a dot of flour off her chin. "He didn't tell me you were coming, either."

Sarah turned away.

She watched Señora Sanchez dancing around the kitchen. "We need *bailarinas* at the *fiesta*," Señora Sanchez said.

Anna began to sift faster.

Sarah stared down at the bowl of apples.

Benjamin opened his mouth.

My fault, he should be saying to Sarah. But he couldn't get the words out.

Señora Sanchez gave Benjamin three eggs. "Crack these into this other bowl," she said.

Adam knelt up higher on the stool. "Benjamin always breaks—" He covered his mouth with one hand.

Benjamin shut his eyes. He smashed the first egg against the bowl.

"*Maravilloso,*" Señora Sanchez said.

There it was, a nice egg with a round yellow yolk, without one piece of eggshell.

He tried the next one.

It didn't work as well.

Bits of shell were mixed in with the eggs.

Señora Sanchez smiled. "*No pasó nada,*" she said. She went to the refrigerator for another egg. "*Otro huevo,*" she said.

Benjamin stood there, helping.

He pictured telling Sarah. They'd call him a *chivo* . . . they'd never be friends . . . and what would Señora Sanchez think?

It took a long time to finish the empanadas.

Señora Sanchez chopped fruit and rolled out the pastry.

Adam and Thomas ate bits of the apple, and Erica rolled a tiny empanada of her own.

At last the pieces of dough were sizzling on the stove.

"I'm glad that's over," said Anna. "I feel like a fried empanada myself."

Everyone laughed.

Even Sarah smiled a little. "I guess we're finished now," she said.

Benjamin looked around at all of them.

"Wait," he said. "I have to tell you something."

When he was finished talking, everyone was quiet for a moment.

Then Anna was telling Sarah she was sorry, and Sarah was laughing. Señora Sanchez began to yell. "*¡Caramba!* I've burned the empanadas again."

Receta para empanadas—ingredientes (reh-SEH-tah PAH-rah ehm-pah-NAH-dahs een-greh-DYEHN-tehs)	Recipe for Empanadas— Ingredients
1½ tazas de harina (TAH-sahs deh ah-REE-nah)	1½ cups of flour
1 cucharadita de levadura (koo-chah-rah-DEE-tah deh leh-vah-DOO-rah)	1 teaspoon of baking powder
3 cucharadas de mantequilla (koo-chah-RAH-dahs deh man-teh-KEE-yah)	3 tablespoons of butter
2 cucharadas de aceite (koo-chah-RAH-dahs deh ah-SAY-teh)	2 tablespoons of cooking oil
1 cucharadita de agua (koo-chah-rah-DEE-tah deh AH-gwah)	1 teaspoon of water
3 huevos (ooEH-vohs)	3 eggs
2 manzanas (en trocitos) (mahn-SAH-nahs ehn troh-SEE-tohs)	2 apples (cut up)
azúcar y canela (ah-SOO-kahr EE kah-NEH-lah)	sugar and cinnamon

Receta para empanadas— instrucciones
(reh-SEH-tah PAH-rah ehm- pah-NAH-dahs een-strook-SYOH-nehs)

Recipe for Empanadas— Instructions

Ask your *madre* or another grown-up to help you.

1. Preheat the oven to 400.

2. Put flour and baking powder into a bowl.

3. Add butter. Use a table knife to cut it into tiny pieces. Then use two knives to mix it into the flour and baking powder.

4. Add cooking oil.

5. Add water and beaten eggs, and mix.

6. Sprinkle flour on a board.

7. Roll the dough on the board until it is flat.

8. Cut 4-inch circles. (You can use a glass.)

9. Grease a baking sheet.

10. Put pieces of cut-up apple, a little sugar, and cinnamon in the center.

11. Fold the circles in half. Glue the edges with a little water. Press the edges together with a fork.

12. Bake for about 25 minutes.

Benjamin could hear music as soon as he opened his apartment door.

Mrs. Muñoz from the library had brought her Spanish CDs to the *fiesta*.

He could see her at one end of the block. Her cart was filled with books. "Don't forget the library," she was calling.

Benjamin could smell something wonderful, too.

Mannie was cooking onions and meat on a grill.

Tortillas were piled high on a counter in front of him.

Anna and Sarah came down the street. They were wearing their long dresses again.

They had spent every minute of yesterday practicing their *baile.*

Benjamin looked down at Mrs. Ortiz's drum in his hand.

He had spent every minute practicing with them.

"Serves you right, *chivo,*" they had both told him.

"*Payaso,*" Sarah had said. "Clown."

But they had been laughing.

And Adam had been calling him *payaso* every two minutes ever since.

And they were friends again.

And playing the drum wasn't so bad after all.

They had spent last night doing something else . . . working on a surprise for Señora Sanchez.

Down the street, Mrs. Ortiz was pouring glasses of *agua de panela*. It was a drink she remembered from Colombia.

Benjamin took a sip. It tasted like water with lots of brown sugar.

"*¡Me gusta!* More, *por favor*," Adam kept saying.

Señora Sanchez was coming down the street toward them. "Too bad about the empanadas," she said, and shook her head. "What's a Spanish *fiesta* without them?"

Then she looked at her watch. "Time for the *baile*?" she asked, smiling.

The three of them looked at each other. "Not yet," Sarah said.

Anna shook her head. "No."

Benjamin looked around.

Spring Street was crowded with people.

Everyone must have seen the signs.

Mrs. Halfpenny was there, and some of the kids from their class.

People from Higby Avenue were there, too.

At one end of the street, Anna's father was playing ball with some of the kids.

At the other end, a line of kids were waiting for Señora Sanchez to paint their faces.

People were dropping money into a big barrel that John from the delicatessen had rolled outside.

There were pennies, and quarters from the kids . . . and lots of dollars from the grown-ups.

It was a good thing.

They couldn't wait for that *piscina* much longer.

Right now, someone was calling their names. "Sarah . . . Anna . . . Benjamin."

Benjamin looked up. Who . . . ?

The street was so crowded, he couldn't see.

"She's here," Sarah was saying.

Benjamin stood on tiptoes.

Coming down the street was a large woman.

She was carrying a huge picnic basket.

Benjamin knew who the woman was. Her glasses were crooked, and a wisp of hair was over her ear.

It was Señora Sanchez's *prima*, Cousin Mercedes, from Spanish Harlem.

Then Señora Sanchez saw her.

She dropped the little bottle of paint she had been holding and ran toward her cousin.

They were both talking and laughing.

"When the children called last night . . . ," Mercedes began.

"A million Estévezes in the phone book . . . ," said Anna.

"And they said you needed empanadas . . . ," Mercedes said.

"I burned every single . . . ," Señora Sanchez said.

"And now," said Sarah, "I think it's time for the *baile*."

Benjamin nodded. He reached for the drum. "*¡Vámonos!*"

BENJAMIN'S SPANISH NOTES

Expresiones **(ehks-preh-SYOH-nehs)**	**Expressions**
¡Qué calor! *(KEH kah-LOHR)*	How hot! (weather)
¡Qué divertido! *(KEH dee-vehr-TEE-doh)*	What fun!
¡Qué maravilloso! *(KEH mah-rah-vee-YOH-soh)*	How marvelous!
Me gusta . . . *(MEH GOOS-tah)*	I like . . .
¡No pasó nada! *(NOH pah-SOH NAH-dah)*	Nothing (bad) happened!
Muy importante. *(MOOee eem-pohr-TAHN-* *teh)*	Very important.
¡Socorro! *(soh-KOH-rroh)*	Help!
Por favor. *(POHR fah-VOHR)*	Please.
¡Vámonos! *(VAH-moh-nohs)*	Come on! Let's go.

Patricia Reilly Giff is the author of many fine books for children, including the Kids of the Polk Street School books, The Lincoln Lions Band books, The Polka Dot Private Eye books, and the New Kids at the Polk Street School books. She lives in Weston, Connecticut.

DyAnne DiSalvo-Ryan has illustrated numerous books for children, including some she has written herself. She lives in Haddonfield, New Jersey.